# Firebright and the
# Magic Medicine

## Daisy Meadows

# For Bea Platt

## ✦ ★ ✦

# Special thanks to Valerie Wilding

ORCHARD BOOKS

First published in Great Britain in 2021 by The Watts Publishing Group

1 3 5 7 9 10 8 6 4 2

Text copyright © 2021 Working Partners Limited
Illustrations © Orchard Books 2021
Series created by Working Partners Limited

A CIP catalogue record for this book is available from the British Library.

ISBN 978 1 40836 386 7

Printed and bound in Great Britain by Clays Ltd, Elcograf S.p.A.

The paper and board used in this book are made from wood from responsible sources.

Orchard Books
An imprint of Hachette Children's Group
Part of The Watts Publishing Group Limited
Carmelite House
50 Victoria Embankment
London EC4Y 0DZ

An Hachette UK Company

www.hachette.co.uk
www.hachettechildrens.co.uk

Contents

Aisha and Emily are best friends from Spellford Village. Aisha loves sports, whilst Emily's favourite thing is science. But what both girls enjoy more than anything is visiting Enchanted Valley and helping their unicorn friends, who live there.

Rosymane

Rosymane is the first of the Healing Crystal Unicorns, whose magical lockets help to keep all the creatures of Enchanted Valley feeling well.

Firebright's special healing magic looks after the inside of the body – everything from a cold to a tummy ache.

Firebright

Twinkleshade

Twinkleshade's healing crystal has the power to soothe worries away and help everyone feel calm.

Ripplestripe uses her amazing magic to heal the heart. She helps to mend friendships after arguments.

Ripplestripe

Spellford

Enchanted Valley

Enchanted Cottage

Golden Palace

An Enchanted Valley lies a twinkle away,
Where beautiful unicorns live, laugh and play.
You can visit the mermaids, or go for a ride,
So much fun to be had, but dangers can hide!

Your friends need your help – this is how you know:
A keyring lights up with a magical glow.
Whirled off like a dream, you won't want to leave.
Friendship forever, when you truly believe.

## Chapter One
# Trouble in Shinehigh Mountains

Aisha Khan pounced on a twig that lay in the long grass beside the River Spell. "Perfect!" she cried, running to join her best friend, Emily Turner, on Spellford Bridge.

They leaned against the wall, holding

their sticks over the water. "Ready?" said Emily. "One, two – three!"

Playing pooh sticks in the bright sunshine was fun. The girls dropped their sticks into the river at exactly the same time. But before Emily or Aisha had a chance to look over the other side of the bridge, they heard joyful barking and a great big SPLASH!

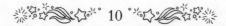

Emily laughed. "It's Feather," she said, pointing at the friendly dog. "He's jumped in after his ball." She waved to her next-door neighbour, Mr Pritchett. He and Feather walked along the river every morning.

Mr Pritchett grinned. "Morning, girls!"

Feather grabbed the ball and climbed on to the bank. He shook himself, spraying silvery droplets everywhere. Then he sneezed. "Woo-shoof!"

Everyone laughed.

"Come on, Feather," said Mr Pritchett. "You need a rub down with a warm towel." He waved to the girls. "Bye!"

"Bye!" they called. Then they leaned over the bridge, to see if their sticks had

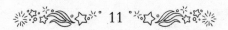

come through the other side. Nothing yet!

"The water's as slow as a sleepy snail," said Aisha.

Emily gasped and pointed to the unicorn keyring dangling from Aisha's belt. "It's glowing!" she said. Her eyes were wide with excitement.

Aisha looked down. Emily's keyring was glowing, too!

When the girls had first explored the attic in Aisha's home, Enchanted Cottage, they'd found a statue of a crystal unicorn. When sunlight struck it, Aisha and Emily were magically transported to a wonderful place called Enchanted Valley, where unicorns lived.

The crystal keyrings were the gift of

Aurora, the unicorn queen. When they glowed, the girls knew she was calling them.

Emily held out her keyring. "I can't wait to see all our friends again," she said.

As well as unicorns, the girls had met pixies, mermaids, dragons and all sorts of magical creatures on their adventures in Enchanted Valley.

Aisha held her keyring close to Emily's. The crystal unicorns sparkled in the sunshine and she felt a force like a strong magnet pulling them together.

When the unicorns touched, the air filled with dazzling sparkles that swirled slowly at first, then faster and faster. The girls felt their feet leave the ground, and they clutched each other in delight.

"We're off for a new adventure!" cried Aisha.

A whirl of brilliant colour surrounded them. Moments later, their toes touched firm ground, and the swirling sparkles slowed and faded.

"We're back in Enchanted Valley!"
Emily said.

They found themselves standing on lush grass at the foot of a hill. A magnificent golden palace stood at the top, with tall twisting turrets like unicorn horns. Sunlight gleamed off the golden roof and pink flowers rambled over the walls.

Three unicorns cantered over the silver drawbridge and headed downhill. The girls waved. They were thrilled to see their friends again.

The first unicorn wore a delicate silver crown, and her glossy coat shifted from pink to red and red to orange in the sunshine, just like the colours of a summer dawn. Her mane and tail shone like gold.

"Welcome!" she said in a soft voice.

"Hello, Queen Aurora!" the girls chorused.

The second unicorn was pure white with a mane and tail of shining silver. His crown had sparkling crystal droplets that flashed rainbow colours in the sunshine. He was the Crystal King and he was visiting Enchanted Valley for a very special occasion: the Crystal Festival!

"We're so glad you're back," he said.

"We are, too!" said Aisha. She turned to the third unicorn, whose coat glowed with the orange colour of apricots. "Hello, Firebright. Oh dear, you still haven't got your locket back."

Each unicorn from Enchanted Valley

wore a magical locket, which helped them to keep their world happy, healthy and peaceful. Queen Aurora looked after the friendships of the valley with the help of her locket. But a wicked unicorn called Selena had stolen Firebright's locket, along with those of the other three Healing Crystal Unicorns. Selena refused to give the lockets back until she was made queen of Enchanted Valley.

Aisha and Emily had vowed never to let that happen.

"You girls helped return Rosymane's Outside healing crystal," Queen Aurora said, "so bumps and bruises are no problem now. But Selena still has Firebright's Inside healing crystal, so there will be lots of nasty coughs and colds unless she gets it back."

The Crystal King spoke up, too. "Selena has Twinkleshade's Head healing crystal,' he said. His horn dipped in sadness. "So we can't be sure of happiness in the valley."

"We love harmony," said Firebright, "but without Ripplestripe's Heart healing crystal there won't be much of that." Her shoulders drooped. "The Crystal Festival can't go ahead if we don't get our lockets back. That will be very bad for the health of everyone in Enchanted Valley."

The girls knew that all the crystals of the valley needed to be recharged in the magical Crystal Festival once a year, or

the magic would be lost for ever.

"How soon is the Crystal Festival?"
Aisha asked.

"It's in two days," said Firebright.

Emily hugged Firebright's neck and
stroked her red-brown mane. "We're here

to help," she said.

Aisha went to Aurora. "We promise you we'll do *anything* to stop Selena taking your place."

"We hoped you'd say that," said Aurora. "We've had a message from the Woffly

family, who live in the Shinehigh Mountains. Something strange is happening." She gave the Crystal King a troubled glance. "They don't understand it, but it's to do with crystals."

"Aurora and I must stay and guard the palace against Selena," the Crystal King said in a solemn voice. His glance settled on the two girls. "We can't think of better helpers than you."

Emily and Aisha's eyes shone with pride.

"Will you go to the Shinehigh Mountains with Firebright?" asked Aurora. "Will you talk to the Woffly family and find out what's happening?" She leaned forward. "Please?"

The girls each put a hand on her velvety-soft nose. Their eyes glittered with excitement. There was no doubt about their answer.

"We will!" they cried.

# Chapter Two
# Woffly Work

Firebright pranced in delight. "I knew you'd say yes," she said. "Jump up!"

The girls had ridden unicorns many times before, but it never stopped being thrilling! They scrambled on to Firebright's back as the king and queen called, "Good luck!"

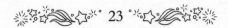

Firebright took off, soaring high above Enchanted Valley. Emily and Aisha squealed with joy as they held on tight. It was so exciting to look down on woods and lakes and meadows.

Emily waved to pixies gathering cloudberries in the treetops, then ducked as a swarm of baby dragons flew overhead, giggling and trying to spit sparks.

They crossed a watery wilderness, and headed towards a range of tall mountains. Sunlight gleamed off snowy peaks that shone white and bright.

"The Shinehighs!" Firebright called.

"I can see where they got their name!" Aisha shouted back.

Forests covered the nearest mountain, and silvery streams and waterfalls tumbled down its slopes. Little wooden cabins stood among the trees.

As they drew closer, Firebright said, "See the cabin with sunnysuckle flowers around a red door? That's where we're heading."

Firebright landed on the grass near a cabin in a clearing beside a stream.

As Aisha jumped down, she noticed glowing colours in the water. "Look," she said in surprise. "Crystals!"

The cabin door creaked open, and four furry creatures came out. They were about half the girls' height, and looked a lot like guinea pigs, except that they had little piggy noses.

"They're adorable," Emily whispered.

"They're guinea hoglets," Firebright whispered back. Aloud, she said, "This is Mr Woffly and Mrs Woffly."

The taller guinea hoglets shook hands with the girls.

"The twins are Wendy and Walt," Firebright finished.

Walt's fur was the colour of gingerbread men, while Wendy's was slightly paler, like runny honey.

Aisha waved. "Hello! I'm Aisha, and this is my friend, Emily. We've come with Firebright to find out what's going on."

"Thank you!" said Mrs Woffly. "We're so worried. You see, every family in

Enchanted Valley should have a set of four
healing crystals."

"They match the lockets belonging to
Firebright and her three unicorn friends,"
Walt added.

Mr Woffly nodded. "And the magic
of the Healing Crystal Unicorns flows
through them. Every year there are new
families who need crystal sets," he said.
"Making sure they get them in time for
the Crystal Festival is Woffly work."

"So we only have two days," Wendy squeaked.

"A-a-woosha!" Walt sneezed.

"Bless you!" Mr Woffly passed him a handkerchief. Then he turned to the girls with a worried frown. "We're searching the stream for crystals, but there are hardly any to be found. And the river seems smaller too."

Emily glanced at Aisha. "How odd," she said.

"We'll help you search for crystals," Aisha told the guinea hoglets.

Emily pointed to some nets with long handles leaning against the cabin. "Do we use those?"

"Yes," said Mrs Woffly. "We scoop up

stones from the riverbed, then pick out the crystals. When they're washed they sparkle like little stars."

"Ooh, gorgeous!" said Emily.

While the older guinea hoglets fetched nets and pans, Wendy touched Aisha's hand. "Do you know where the crystals come from?" she asked shyly.

The girls shook their heads.

"Whenever a magical rainbow ends over Enchanted Valley," said Wendy, "little pieces of it fall to earth. Most turn into flowers, but if they land in our river, they turn into coloured crystals."

Walt said proudly, "Wendy and I are collecting crystals for the first time this year." His whiskers drooped. "But we haven't found many yet. It's strange."

As Wendy bent to help a bumble-beetle over a pebble, Aisha whispered to Emily, "Could this be Selena's work?"

Before Aisha could reply, Walt sneezed again. "A-a-woosha!" He sneezed so hard he tumbled backwards, making everyone laugh.

Mr Woffly handed nets to Aisha and Emily. "Don't fall in!" he said with a wink and a smile.

"We'll be careful," Emily promised.

The girls swished their nets in the stream, then lifted them out and picked out the few crystals amongst the stones. Then they put them in Mrs Woffly's special crystal bowl for rinsing.

"A-a-woosha!" Walt's huge sneeze made his body shake like shivery jelly.

Firebright asked quietly, "Are you feeling OK?"

Walt dabbed his little piggy nose with the handkerchief. "Fine, thanks. It's just the sneezles."

Emily noticed a locket hanging around Walt's neck. "That's pretty," she said. "I thought only unicorns had lockets."

"They're the – a-a-woosha! – only ones with *magic* lockets," said Walt. "This one isn't magical. I made it for my friend, Rain. It's her birthday today."

The locket held a tiny flower with petals of different colours.

"It's very pretty," said Aisha. "It even has a drop of dew on it."

"A-a-woosha! It's not dew," said Walt. "I caught a raindrop, because that matches Rain's name."

Wendy bounced up and down. "We're going to her pool party in the lagoon later," she said.

Walt patted his locket. "I can't wait to give her my present."

Mrs Woffly brought her bowl over. "Any more crystals?" she asked.

There weren't.

Emily took Aisha aside. "Why are there suddenly so few crystals in—" She stopped. Something further upstream caught her eye. A long, slinky creature was darting around – a creature she'd seen before.

"Uh-oh," she said. "Is that Slick?"

Slick was a naughty otter, who'd been helping Selena with her horrible plans.

Aisha shaded her eyes with a hand. "It *is* Slick," she gasped. "And I bet he's stealing crystals!"

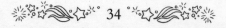

# Chapter Three
# A Warning for Slick

The Woffly family came to see what was happening.

Aisha pointed upstream. "Watch that otter. He's up to no good."

Slick leaped out of the river, clutching something in his paw.

"What's he doing?" asked Mrs Woffly.

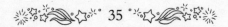

Emily stared, eyes wide, as she spotted flashes of colour coming from Slick's paws. "Crystals! He's got crystals!" She grabbed Aisha's hand. "He's taking them! No wonder you've been struggling to find any."

The otter stuffed the crystals into a bulging net bag.

Aisha headed upstream along the bank, shouting, "Slick!"

The naughty creature turned. "Hee hee!" he laughed, then stuck out his tongue.

Emily gasped. "That's so rude!" she cried. "Give those crystals to Mr and Mrs Woffly right now!"

Slick blew a loud raspberry. "*Thhhbbpp!*"

Aisha started to tell
him off when a flash
of lightning made her
jump. It was followed
by a violent crash of
thunder. At the same
time, there was a cry
from Walt as he fell into the river!

"Hold on, I'm coming!" Emily cried.
She kneeled on the bank and, as Walt
surfaced, she stretched out and grabbed
his paw. He spluttered and coughed as she
pulled him to safety.

As Emily stood Walt on the bank,
another zap of lightning made the grass
behind them crackle and smoke.

Wendy squealed and ran to her parents.

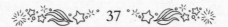

Walt hid behind the girls.

Emily and Aisha's hearts pounded. They clutched hands as the smoke cleared to reveal a silver unicorn with purple eyes, and a dark blue mane and tail. She gave an evil, cackling laugh.

"Selena!" cried Emily.

The bad unicorn stamped her hooves,

sending sparks in all directions.

"What are you doing here?" Aisha demanded. "Stirring up trouble?"

Selena's eyes narrowed. She turned to the guinea hoglets, who cowered together. Their whiskers quivered. "Don't bother fishing for crystals, you silly furballs," she sneered. "They're useless without the magic of the Healing Crystal lockets. Those unicorns and their foolish friends will never get them back."

Aisha was furious. "We will!" she said.

Selena glared. "You won't! Not until I'm queen of Enchanted Valley."

"We'll never let that happen," Emily said, "and you know it."

Walt shivered and huddled between

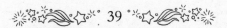

the girls. Aisha dabbed water droplets off his little piggy nose. "Don't worry," she whispered. "We've stopped Selena's horrid plans before. We'll stop her again."

"Ha!" said Selena. She glanced upstream to where Slick stood watching. "My little otter looks busy. Slick!" she shouted. "Come here! Now!"

The otter swam downriver and leaped on to the bank. He smirked, and opened his paw to show Selena a green crystal.

"You're stealing more things, I see," she said. "Good, good! But you haven't forgotten your important task, have you? The locket I gave you to look after – it had better be safe!"

"I've kept it safe!" said Slick, looking a

little annoyed. "It's in—"

"Quiet, you foolish otter!" Selena snapped. "Don't tell them where it is! Just make sure they don't find it."

Mumbling crossly, the silver unicorn leaped into the air amid lightning flashes and crashes of thunder.

As soon as she'd gone, Slick dived to the bottom of the stream and came up clutching something. "Hee hee," he giggled. "I'll take this too." He opened his paw and held up a locket. It had a tiny raindrop in the middle.

Walt gasped. "Rain's locket. It must have come off when I fell in the water." He scurried to Slick. "Give it back! I made that for my friend!" he said.

Slick poked his tongue out again. "Mine now!" he said. Then he dived into the water and swam upstream.

"He's so mean!" said Aisha.

Firebright pawed the ground. "That bad otter has not only hidden my locket," she said, "he's stolen Rain's birthday present too."

"We'll put things right," said Aisha. "Won't we, Emily?"

Emily hugged Walt close as he sniffled and shivered. "We will," she promised. "We have to!"

If they didn't, the health of everyone in Enchanted Valley was in danger.

# Chapter Four
# After That Otter!

Wendy fetched a blanket, while Mr and Mrs Woffly put their crystals away safely.

The girls desperately wanted to make everything right, but all they could do for now was help Wendy wrap Walt in the warm, fluffy blanket.

Walt gave an enormous sneeze. "A-a-woosha! A-a-woosha!"

"Oh no!" cried Firebright. "He was sneezing when we arrived. He's getting a cold, and I can't make him better without my locket!" Her eyes glistened with tears. "I can't bear it if I can't help!"

"It's not your fault. It's Selena's!" said Aisha. "But we'll fix it. We'll get your locket back." She pressed her face against Firebright's soft cheek, thinking, *Somehow*.

"Come indoors, Walt," said Mr Woffly. "You can't go to Rain's party with a cold." He lifted the little guinea hoglet into his arms.

Walt's sad face peered over his dad's shoulder. "I've been looking forward to her party for ages," he said.

"Leave it to us, Walt," Emily told him.

"I'll help, too." Wendy blew her twin a kiss. "You mustn't miss the party."

Walt smiled bravely as he was carried indoors to bed.

The girls huddled together with Firebright and Wendy. "Let's watch Slick and see if we can find a clue to where he's hidden Firebright's locket," Aisha suggested.

Everyone agreed this was a good idea, so they all made their way quietly upstream. There were plenty of tree trunks to dodge behind. They stopped for a moment and watched Slick dive underwater. He came up with a large red crystal, and popped it in his net bag.

"Why does he want them?" Emily wondered.

Slick flipped over and swam upstream on his back, with the bag of crystals resting on his tummy.

"Follow him," whispered Firebright.

The otter had disappeared around a bend, and the friends raced along the bank until they spotted him again.

They ducked behind a huge boulder and Emily peeped out to see what Slick was doing. She saw a huge heap of branches, rocks and sticks piled up in the river – half in the water, half out. "He's building himself a den!" she whispered. "See? It even has a little front door made of tree bark."

Sunshine glinted off the den. Brilliant colours flashed from it. Aisha was the first to realise why.

"He's covering his den in crystals!" she said. "That's why he's been collecting them!"

Slick clambered up on to the roof. He opened the net bag and took out his new red crystal. He placed it carefully on the roof, but it rolled away. He caught it and tried again.

"The water level beyond the den looks much higher than on this side," said Firebright.

Emily frowned. "The den must be holding water back, like a dam."

Wendy gasped, "That's why the river near our cabin is just a stream. Mum and Dad will be so cross with Slick."

Emily's hand flew to her mouth. "Look!"

she said, and pointed to where a glimmer of bright orange shone through the den's open door. "That's—"

"My locket!" cried Firebright.

"Hush, everyone," said Aisha. "This is our chance to get it back."

Wendy led the way, but as she rounded a small boulder, her paw slipped on loose stones. "Oops!" she cried.

Slick spun around. "Who's that? A hoglet! What do you want?"

The others caught up with Wendy.

"Slick, I need my locket," Firebright said. "It makes sick creatures better."

"And we need the locket Walt made too," Wendy squeaked. "Please?"

The naughty otter scowled. "No," he

said. "I want colourful things for my den.
I'm making the roof all the colours of
the rainbow." He clutched his net bag.
"I never had anything pretty before. Go
away."

He carried on putting crystals on his
den.

Aisha hugged Wendy. "I know you want
to rescue Walt's locket," she said, "but it's
important that we get Firebright's locket
back first."

"But how?" wondered Emily.

Wendy jumped up. "Me!" she said. "I'm
small enough to get through the den door.
I'll creep inside and take the locket."

Firebright nuzzled the little hoglet's
cheek. "You're very brave," she said, "but

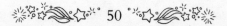

you can't reach the
door from the
riverbank."

They had
another think.
Then Emily
said, "I've got a
plan! Aisha and
Firebright, you distract
Slick so he doesn't see what Wendy
and I are up to."

Wendy gave an excited little jump.
"What *are* we up to?"

Emily grinned. "I'll lift you over to the
doorway. Then you can grab the locket!
How's that?"

Aisha wasn't sure. "Are you brave

enough to do that, Wendy?"

The little guinea hoglet puffed up her fur and lifted her chin. "I certainly am," she said. "I'll do it for Queen Aurora and for Firebright." She took a deep breath and carried on. "I'll also do it for the other Healing Crystal Unicorns, and my brother, and for every creature in the whole of Enchanted Valley!"

Firebright gazed down at her. "Wendy, you're wonderful!"

The little hoglet's piggy nose turned pink with pride.

Aisha and Emily swept her into an enormous hug. They had a plan. Now to put it into action!

# Chapter Five
# Aisha Makes a Deal

Aisha and Firebright had to get to the far side of the den. They crept through the trees until they were further upstream than Slick. Then they turned around and, with the unicorn's hooves clopping loudly over the stones, they drew near to the den.

Slick looked up from his work on the

roof. "What do you want?" he asked.

"We just want to talk," said Firebright.

Aisha slipped off the unicorn's back and stepped closer, but Slick held up a paw and scowled. "Keep away," he said. "You're not getting your locket back."

Aisha spotted Emily and Wendy. They were behind Slick, creeping towards his den. She knew she had to keep the otter's attention. "You see, Slick," she said, "your den's blocking—"

"My den's lovely!" he said.

"It's certainly a beautiful den," Firebright said. "It must have taken ages to build."

Aisha held her breath. Behind Slick's back, Emily picked up Wendy.

"Actually, I'm an amazingly fast builder," Slick boasted. "It's taken hardly any time at all, and now I'm smothering the roof with crystals!"

Aisha saw Emily leaning over the water to lower Wendy down to the door. But her foot knocked a large pebble into the water. *Splash!*

Quickly, Aisha coughed to cover up the sound.

But Slick still heard it. He spun round. "Stop!" he yelled, as he scrambled over the top of his den towards the others.

Wendy gave a frightened squeal, and clung to Emily's arm as she was lifted back to the safety of the bank.

Aisha sighed in relief. At least their

little friend was safe, even if the plan was ruined.

"Ow!" cried a voice. It was Slick! His paw had caught on a long, thick branch. It shifted sideways, and nudged a small rock.

The rock moved.

The branch rolled.

The whole den quaked.

Slick's new home was collapsing beneath his paws!

A big hole appeared in the back wall of the den. Now there was nothing holding the water back! It gushed and gurgled through in frothy waves.

"Run, Slick!" cried Firebright. "Everyone stand clear!"

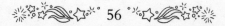

A torrent of water flooded through the den, making it crash down into pieces. Slick tried to leap clear of the falling branches and rocks. His paws slithered and scrabbled but he didn't make it. With a great splash he landed in the rushing water among the sticks from the den.

Emily stretched out her body and made a desperate grab for Slick's leg. "Hold on!" she cried. Her hand closed around his smooth, glossy tummy and she pulled

him back to safety on the bank.

Everyone was OK, and that was all that mattered.

Slick shook himself and wiped water from his eyes.

Instead of thanking Emily, he snapped, "Look what you've all done! You've ruined my lovely, colourful den!"

"We didn't!" Aisha said. "*You* kicked that branch, not us. You ruined it yourself."

Firebright lowered her head and said softly, "Please, Slick, give me my locket."

"No!" said the otter. He turned his back and sat down with a very cross "Chah!'

"You'd make Queen Aurora and the Healing Crystal Unicorns very happy if you gave it back," said Emily.

Firebright nodded. "So many creatures have coughs and colds," he said. "Like poor Walt. I'd make them better if I had my locket."

"Too bad!" said Slick.

Aisha and Emily knew he was probably scared of what Selena would do if he gave the locket back.

Wendy padded over to Slick. "What if we brought you lots of colourful things?" she asked. "Would you give back the locket then?"

The otter was quiet for a moment. The friends held their breath.

"Perhaps," said Slick, "if you help me rebuild my den – and make it really colourful. But you'd need to make it even

more beautiful than before." He looked
at them sternly. "Maybe then it would be
worth giving back a locket."

The girls grinned.

"It's a deal!" Aisha said happily. "A den
for a locket – shake on it?" She held out
her hand and, after a second or two, Slick
put his paw in it, and they shook. Aisha
didn't mind his cold, wet fur at all. Slick
had agreed!

"We'll be back soon!" cried Emily, as she climbed on to Firebright's back. "Gather some fresh branches, Slick!"

Aisha lifted Wendy up so she snuggled close to Emily, then she climbed on. The unicorn leaped into the air, and away they flew to search.

Firebright was upset to hear coughs and sneezes echoing around Enchanted Valley below. Aisha stroked her velvety neck. "Don't worry, Firebright," she said. "We just need to collect brightly coloured things, then you'll have your locket back."

"But listen ..." said Firebright sadly.

"Ka-a-shoo!" sneezed a bob-tailed squirrel.

"A-choo!" came a sneeze from a mouse

among the trees below.

"A-woosh! Sniff! Sniff!"

"I'm hot!"

"A-choo! I'm cold!"

"Oh no!" cried Wendy. "Everyone's getting sick."

Emily whispered in Aisha's ear, "We really need to get Firebright's locket back! And soon!"

## Chapter Six
# Waving Mermaids

As Firebright flew over Enchanted
Valley, Aisha spotted some old friends
in a meadow below. "There's Ember the
phoenix with her chicks," she said. "But
something's wrong. They're huddled
together."

"Let's take a look," said Firebright. She

glided down to land beside the birds.

Ember sneezed. "Choo!"

"Ch-choo! Ch-choo!" sneezed the chicks.

The girls and Wendy jumped down and ran to Ember. The phoenix's glorious red and orange tail feathers were floppy, and her orange crest drooped.

"We've caught colds," said Ember. "Firebright, can you help?"

Aisha quickly explained that Selena had stolen the Healing Crystal Unicorns' lockets. She told Ember about Slick's den, and how they needed to gather colourful objects for him so he'd give Firebright's locket back.

"I can help!" Ember immediately

plucked two bright feathers from her tail
and handed them over with a flourish.

"Thank you!" said Emily, who had
a lap full of snuggling, sneezing chicks.
"That's a brilliant start to our collection."

"You're welcome," said Ember, "and I have an idea. My chicks and I will fly around telling everyone what you need. The fresh air will do us good. Ready, little ones? Spread wings!"

"Check!" said the chicks.

"Beaks forward!"

"Check!"

"Flap away!" said Ember.

"Ch-choo! Ch-choo! Ch-check!"

With sneezes and sniffles, they were off.

"Where next?" asked Wendy.

"The mermaids' lagoon!" said Emily. "Mermaids love brightly coloured things."

A few minutes later, Firebright landed by the shore of the lagoon. There, sitting on a rock, were two little mermaids. One looked up and waved.

"Aisha and Emily!" she called in
a tinkling voice. Her sweet face was
surrounded by a tangled mass of purple,
blue and pink hair.

"It's Pearl!" said Emily.

The girls were delighted to see their
friend again, but sorry to see the second
little mermaid's head was drooping.

"What's wrong?" asked Aisha.

Firebright nuzzled beneath the
mermaid's silky green-gold hair. "Rain?"
she said. "What's wrong?"

The mermaid leaned her head against
the unicorn's nose.

"Wendy's here," said Firebright, "and so
are my friends, Aisha and Emily."

Rain looked up and coughed. "Sorry, I'm feeling sad. I've caught a nasty cold on my birthday."

Emily hugged her, just as four white creatures broke through the surface of the water. Their silvery manes were dull, as if they had lost their shine. The girls thought

they were ponies, until they noticed the creatures had mermaid tails.

"It's the kelpies," said Pearl. "And they don't look well either."

One kelpie coughed, and the others sneezed.

"Oh no," said Emily. "They're ill, too."

There was the sound of running feet, and a goblin with a wrinkly green face hurried towards them. He held his pointy hat on with one hand and waved with the other.

"Hob!" Aisha cried in delight. The goblin had helped them on several of their adventures.

Hob skidded to a stop. "I've brought some Cough Dewdrops for the birthday

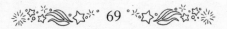

mermaid!" he said, and fished out a large bag of lozenges. "Only the Healing Crystal Unicorns can cure you," he told Rain, "but this will make you feel better." He gave her one, and one each to the kelpies. They whinnied softly as their throats cleared, and they brightened a little.

Aisha told Hob and Rain why they were at the lagoon, and how they planned to get Firebright's locket back.

"Then she'll cure everyone!" Emily added.

Rain slipped into the water, and dipped her head below the surface. Aisha and Emily heard her give a rippling, musical call. Moments later, they felt a thrill as

lots of smiling mermaids appeared. Their
hair floated on the water like the most
delicate seaweed as they waved. "Hello,
girls. Hi, Wendy and Firebright!"

The girls ran to the water's edge. The
mermaids clutched handfuls of coloured
shells, and brightly patterned hair combs.

"These are for Slick," Rain said.

Pearl bobbed to the surface and held out a handful of pearls in all the colours of the rainbow, but before anyone could thank the mermaids, the kelpies reappeared and dropped chunks of emerald coral on the shore.

"That's great, thank you all!" said Emily.

Suddenly, they heard the wind whistling above their heads.

Aisha looked up. "It's Ember and her chicks!" she cried.

The phoenix had brought some bright pink candy. "It's from Surly the troll," she said. "He wants to help get Firebright's locket back."

The chicks carried bunches of red and

purple everlasting blossoms. "They're from Flowerdew Garden," Ember said. "Primrose the gnome said if you sprinkle them with water and say 'Nibble nubble, blossoms double', you'll have twice as many!"

"Fantastic!" said Wendy, wiggling her little piggy nose in delight.

Aisha gave some Cough Dewdrops to Ember and the chicks. They flew off to tell more creatures about the plan to get the locket back.

Hob returned with a large basket bobbing in front of him. He sat down to catch his breath and his hat flopped over one eye. "These are for you!" he said, showing them lots of coloured bottles.

"They're quick-drying magical paints."

"Brilliant!" said Firebright. "Thanks, Hob."

"I can't wait to use those," said Wendy. "We'll make everything really colourful."

They had more than enough now! The friends waved goodbye to the mermaids, Hob and the kelpies. Firebright flew them over meadows and forests, straight to the Woffly family's cabin in the Shinehigh Mountains. The girls could hardly believe their eyes – before them was a blaze of colour!

## Chapter Seven
# An Army of Helpers

"Ember, you've done a fantastic job of spreading the word," said Aisha.

The grass was piled high with coloured stones and bottles, beads from old necklaces, and a bag of spare buttons from Buckle the leprechaun. Jolly the elf had brought heaps of coloured crayons

and there were painted nutshells from the girls' football-playing friend Sapling, a wood nymph.

Mrs Woffly filled baskets with the gifts so that Emily, Aisha and Wendy could take them to Slick. Ember and her chicks bounced along on Firebright's back.

"Look what we've got, Slick!" Wendy called.

Emily nudged Aisha. She'd noticed that Slick was wearing both Firebright's locket and the one Walt had made.

The otter's mouth dropped open when he saw the baskets. "Wow!" he said. His whiskers twitched with excitement. "Look, I've gathered lots of strong branches. I can build my new den right across the river."

"No, don't!" said Wendy. "You'll stop the water flowing downstream. Our part of the river will dry up. We'll never find the crystals we need."

Slick scowled. "This den has to be bigger and better than the old one. If it's not, then no locket for you!"

Tears sprang into Wendy's eyes, but Emily whispered, "I've an idea." She

turned to Slick. "Those big branches will support a lot of weight. Let's make an arch in the middle of the den, so the river can flow right through."

Slick thought for a moment, then nodded and clapped his paws! "One end of the den can be my bedroom, on this side of the river," he said. "On the other side, I'll have a room for eating and playing. The arch between them will be my own private bridge."

Emily and Aisha smiled in relief.

Slick and Firebright dragged branches into place to make the arch over the water. Everyone else packed rocks and moss between them.

"Look at Ember's chicks," Aisha giggled.

They were sneezing and painting pebbles with Hob's magical paints. There was striped paint and spotty paint and sparkly star paint. One bottle was labelled 'What-you-want paint'. The chicks had fun with that, and ended up with zigzag pebbles and whirly pebbles and even a patchwork pebble!

"The den needs to be strong to have all those pebbles on the roof," said Emily. She swept her hair off her forehead. "Whew! We need more help."

Aisha pointed to several specks in the sky. "Look!"

The specks grew larger. A whole flight of unicorns was coming towards them, with creatures riding on their backs.

Emily could see sleep pixies and kitterflies flying alongside, too.

As they landed, goblins, pixies and elves jumped down and marched to the den, chattering excitedly.

Emily grinned. "It's like a happy little army!"

"What can we do?" asked a pixie.

Slick's little mouth dropped open.

"You've come to help?"

Aisha smiled. "That's what friends do."

Emily asked the goblins to collect rocks, and the elves to gather pebbles. Aisha showed the pixies how to stuff moss between rocks. The unicorns rested, so they would be fresh for the flight back.

The den grew and grew. Soon, the fun part began – topping the roof with the gifts. Wendy sang as she worked.

"*Pink shells and blue beads and buttons of green,*

*The brightest of colours that we've ever seen.*

*Stick them on, poke them in, pat them and then,*

*Slick will be pleased with his lovely new den.*"

"We hope!" whispered Emily. She and Aisha sang along as they put mermaids' combs and shells into place. They tucked buttons and coral among the rocks, and the chicks placed their painted pebbles around the roof edge.

Everyone stood back to admire the beautiful den and the sparkling water flowing beneath the arch.

Slick clapped his paws. "It's the most brilliant den ever!"

Aisha, Emily, Wendy and Firebright waved goodbye as the unicorns flew off with their friends to get ready for Rain's party.

Emily said to Slick, "It was lovely to see you have fun with everyone."

He looked away, his face falling immediately. "It wasn't fun. I just wanted lots of colourful things and you brought them to me. Hah!"

The friends stared in shock.

"If I wasn't a nice guinea hoglet," Wendy muttered, "I'd knock his den down."

Aisha hugged her. "Well, you are a nice guinea hoglet," she said. "Slick is probably grateful."

"I'm sure he is," said Emily. "Slick, we've kept our part of the bargain. Can we have the locket, please?"

"Of course," he said.

Firebright's eyes brightened and Wendy's piggy nose quivered.

"Here," said Slick. He handed over the locket Walt had made for Rain.

"Thanks," said Aisha, tucking it in her pocket. "But that's not the one you agreed to give back."

Slick smirked. "Actually, I never agreed which one I'd give back. I said I'd give back a locket. I never said *which* locket. Hah!"

The friends gasped. How could the otter be so horrible – just when they'd helped him rebuild his den?

"You cheat!" cried Emily.

Slick blew a raspberry. "*Thhhbbpp!*"

Aisha wondered if she could snatch Firebright's locket, but Slick plunged into the water and swam downstream.

Firebright shook her head. "That's it," she said tearfully. "My locket's gone."

Aisha pulled a mermaid's comb from the den's roof. "Emily, do you remember what these do?"

"Yes," said Emily. "When we put them in our hair, they turn us into mermaids!"

Aisha grinned. "They've given me an idea."

⋆ ⋆

Aisha's strong mermaid tail powered her through the water as she swam after Slick. *I must hurry*, she thought. *I hope the others will be there, waiting.* They'd agreed their plan – Emily and the others would wait by the cabin, further down the river.

She drew closer and made a grab for the locket. But Slick was too slippery and slithery, which was what she'd expected. He swam away from her.

"I'll catch you!" Aisha yelled.

"You won't!" Slick shouted. "I'm speedier than anyone!"

Aisha chased after him, further

downstream. Even though she had a tail to help her swim, Slick was faster.

As he drew near the cabin, Emily, Firebright and Wendy leaped up. Each of them held a net with a long bamboo handle. Slick was streaking towards them and didn't seem to notice that anyone was waiting to pounce. Wendy held her net over the river then, as Slick drew near, she swished it through the water. Left, right, swish, swoosh! But …

"I missed!" she cried.

Emily raced along the bank to keep up with Slick. She grasped her net in both hands and swooped.

"Got him!" she cried.

Slick wriggled, but it was no use. Emily

had caught him.

Wendy and Firebright cheered, "Hooray!"

Aisha was so delighted that she punched a wet fist into the air, rising up on her

glittering mermaid's tail. "Teamwork!" she cried to her friends on the bank.

"Yay!" Emily cried back, waving to her friend.

# Chapter Eight
# Party Time!

Emily reached into the net and took Firebright's locket from around Slick's neck. There was nothing the otter could do to stop her. As he tried to scrabble for the treasure, he tipped sideways and fell back into the river with a plop! "Give me my locket!" he demanded when he

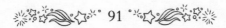

bobbed back up again.

"It's not yours, Slick," Aisha called as she pulled herself ashore. She took the magical comb from her hair. With a shiver and a quiver, her tail disappeared and she returned to normal. Mrs Woffly wrapped her in a fluffy towel.

Emily put the locket around Firebright's neck. It shimmered brilliant orange. "Bright as a summer sunrise!" Emily said.

"Thank you!" said Firebright. "Wendy, fetch Walt and the Woffly crystal set, please."

Wendy scurried away, and returned with her twin, who wore a cosy dressing gown and unicorn slippers. He carried a red box decorated with a glistening silver W.

"A-a-woosha!" Walt sneezed, and opened the box. Tinkling sounds came from inside, like wind chimes in a gentle breeze.

"Take out the Inside crystal," said Firebright.

Walt took out a dull orange crystal. Instantly, it glowed as bright as Firebright's locket. The hoglet's eyes

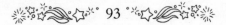

brightened, too. "I've stopped sneezing!
I feel better." He turned to his parents.
"Can I go to the party?"

"Of course!" they said.

Aisha and Emily were glad to see the
Woffly family looking happy at last.

Walt stroked Firebright's velvety coat.
"Thanks for making me better," he said.

The unicorn shook her head. "It's not
me you should thank. It's Aisha, Emily
and Wendy."

"Thanks, everybody!" Walt said happily.
He was even happier when Aisha gave
him back the locket he'd made for Rain.

"Thanks!" he said. "I can't wait to give
it to her."

Emily gave a shout. "The river!" she

cried. "Now Slick's den isn't blocking it,
crystals are travelling in the water again."

It was true! The riverbed sparkled with
colour!

"Hooray!" everyone cheered.

Mrs Woffly grabbed a net. "Get

swishing, Mr Woffly," she squeaked.

"There'll easily be enough for the Crystal Festival," her husband said joyfully. "Every family in Enchanted Valley will have their own set!"

Emily spotted Slick sitting on a tree stump with his back to everyone. "Chah! I lost the locket," he muttered. "Selena will be so cross."

A zap of lightning and crash of thunder made the girls jump. The sky darkened.

"Selena!" cried Aisha. "Run, hoglets!"

The Woffly family scampered into the cabin. Selena swooped down fast, making Firebright and the girls leap aside. Little balls of lightning skittered over her silver body. "Slick!" she screamed. "What

have you done? I told you to guard that locket!"

"I … I … I … they tricked me! They cheated!" he said.

Aisha put her hands on her hips. It was *Slick* who'd tricked *them*!

"You let those silly girls trick you?" Selena said with a snarl. "Don't *ever* disobey me again!"

She reared, and sparks shot from her hooves as they crashed on to a rock.

Slick cowered, covering his eyes.

"I'll be watching for you girls," Selena sneered. "You'll never get the other two lockets back. I will be queen, you'll see!"

Emily lifted her chin. "We'll *never* let that happen. And you know it!"

"Pah!" Selena leaped into the air and disappeared into a dark grey cloud. Lightning crackled.

There was silence. Then …

*Splash!*

Slick jumped into the water, and swam towards his den.

One by one, the Woffly family crept out

from their cabin.

"She's gone!" called Aisha.

"Hooray!" said Walt. His eyes sparkled, and his nose woffled. "It's party time!"

The girls climbed on to Firebright's back. Mr Woffly lifted the twins up to sit between them.

"Bye!" the friends called.

Mr and Mrs Woffly waved. "Have fun!"

Firebright flew low, skimming the treetops. As creatures saw the gleaming orange locket around her neck, they fetched their healing crystals. The sound of sneezes and coughs faded away.

"They'll all be better soon," Firebright said happily.

Firebright gave Rain the best birthday present ever – she cured her cold in time for her party! Excited guests began to arrive from all directions. When Queen Aurora and the Crystal King flew down to the shore, everyone cheered.

Aurora went straight to the girls. "Thank you!" she said. "You've saved Enchanted Valley once again."

"Wendy, too," said the Crystal King.

Aisha nodded. "We'd never have done it without her and Firebright."

Aurora wished Rain a happy birthday, and turned to the guests. "Now that everyone is well, let's have fun!"

Aisha still had her magic comb, and Rain found one for Emily. They plunged into the lagoon and had a great time slapping the water with their pearly tails.

Emily nudged Aisha. "Look at Rain."

Walt was giving her the birthday locket. The girls smiled at the delight on Rain's lovely face.

Rain disappeared underwater for a moment, then shot into the air and turned a triple somersault. "Happiest birthday ever!" she squealed. "Wheeeee!"

She splashed down and she and Walt fell together in a hug, giggling.

There were games next. Aisha won Pass the Pearl, and Wendy easily won Rocky Run. The game everyone loved most was What's for Dinner, Mr Shark? Eddie the kelpie was Mr Shark, and he got everyone screaming in glee.

A pale blue unicorn arrived, wearing a chef's hat. A mother-of-pearl tray floated before him, and on it was a pink cake shaped like a waterlily. Each petal was iced with sweet sea foam and tipped with sparkling gold. A big pearly bubble hovered above tall blue candles.

"Chef Yummytum, that's gorgeous! Thank you!" said Rain.

The chef blew on the bubble. It burst into tiny flames, which dropped like fiery raindrops on to the candles. Everyone sang "Happy Birthday" while Rain made a wish and blew out the candles.

Emily and Aisha removed their magic combs as Chef Yummytum handed the cake around. They had just returned to their proper form, when Emily noticed a small brown figure hiding by some reeds.

"Slick's here!" she said.

Rain saw him, too. "Join the party," she called. "Everyone's welcome!"

"Even naughty otters," whispered Aisha.

But Slick scowled and blew a raspberry. Then, with a flick of his tail, he was gone. Maybe one day he'd be happy to be friends!

Emily shrugged, and nibbled her

cake. "Mmm, it tastes of honey and watermelon …"

"Strawberries and cream," said Pearl.

"Everything I like best!" said Walt.

The girls laughed. Then Aurora said, "I expect you must leave soon, but I want you to know how happy you've made everyone. Aisha, Emily, Firebright, Wendy – you're amazing!"

"So am I," said Walt, through a mouthful of sticky sea foam.

Aurora laughed. "You are!"

Aisha and Emily promised to come back again to help find the last two Healing Crystal lockets. "Bye, everyone, see you soon!" they cried.

Aurora lowered her horn, and filled the

air with sparkles. Their brilliant colours
spun and merged together until the girls
were surrounded by a swirling, whirling
wall of colour. They clasped hands as they
rose upwards. Moments later, they felt
their feet touch firm ground. The sparkles
cleared.

"We're back on Spellford Bridge!" said
Emily.

"No time passes while we're in
Enchanted Valley," said Aisha, "so let's
check on our pooh sticks!" She reached
up on tiptoe and looked over the wall.
"Where are they?"

They ran down on to the riverbank,
and peered beneath the bridge to see if
their sticks were stuck.

"Look!" Emily cried. In the middle of
the river, a little otter swam lazily on his
back. He clutched the two pooh sticks to
his tummy.

"Maybe he'll use them to build a den!"
said Aisha.

"With a grand arch!" Emily added.

They both laughed.

The girls would always remember building a den with a naughty otter and their magical friends.

The End

Join Emily and Aisha
for more fun in ...
# Twinkleshade and the Calming Charm
**Read on for a sneak peek!**

"Good morning, yogis!" A woman in animal-print leggings and a bright orange T-shirt waved from the TV screen. "Are you ready to ...

"Stretch yourself sunny!" Emily's mum joined in with Yogi Yolanda's catchphrase. Aisha and Emily smiled at each other. Emily's mum did these classes every day and was always saying how relaxing they were. The girls had only recently started joining in with the classes and they were loads of fun.

On screen, Yolanda was still talking.

"We'll be doing the downward dog pose, and the happy baby pose – I know you guys love that one! – but first, let's start with a tree pose!"

"Come on, girls," Emily's mum said.

### Read
# Twinkleshade and the Calming Charm
## to find out what's in store
## for Aisha and Emily!

# Also available

**Book Thirteen:**

Rosymane and the Rescue Crystal

**Book Fourteen:**

Firebright and the Magic Medicine

**Book Fifteen:**

Twinkleshade and the Calming Charm

**Book Sixteen:**

Ripplestripe and the Peace Locket

# Unicorn Magic

## Look out for the next book!

If you like
Unicorn Magic,
you'll love …

# Welcome to Animal Ark!

Animal-mad Amelia is sad
about moving house, until she
discovers Animal Ark, where vets look
after all kinds of animals in need.

Join Amelia and her friend Sam for a
brand-new series of animal adventures!